Raela
and the
Magic Wall

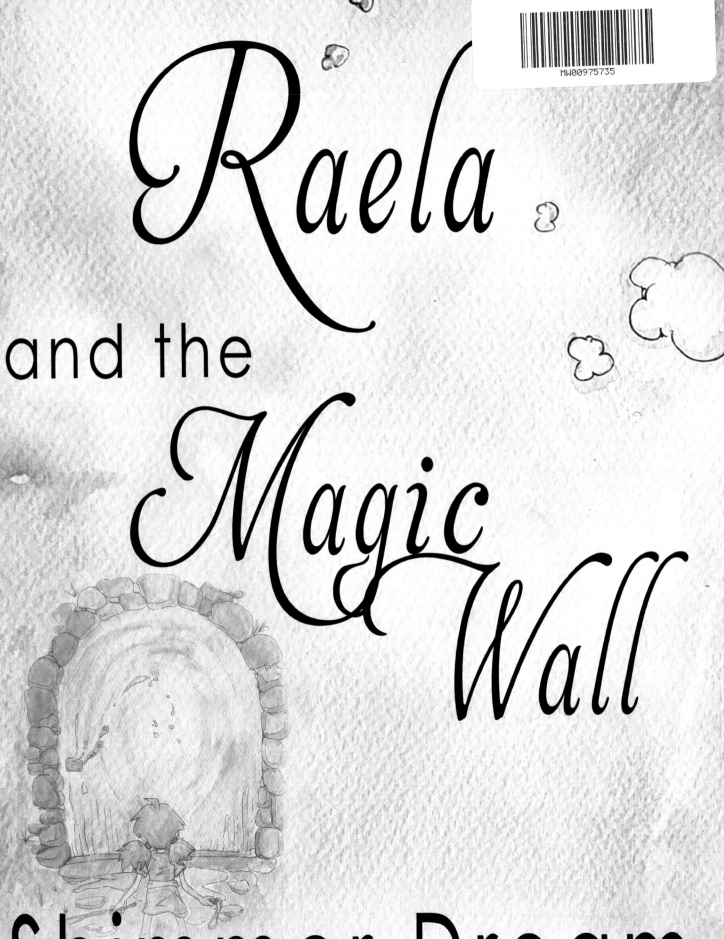

Shimmer Dream

Raela was a young girl who
liked to tell herself stories
about adventures in magical lands.

But no one wanted to listen to them.

Especially her older sister Pearl. She was supposed to watch Raela but spent all her time talking on her phone instead.

When Raela tried to tell Pearl her newest story, she got mad.

"Oh, go outside."

With her head bowed and her shoulders slumped, Raela shuffled out the door."

Raela picked up a stick and doodled in the dirt.

She drew some flowers and then added a figure hiding behind them.

She asked herself what
character she was drawing.
Maybe a goblin girl.

What would she look like?

She wouldn't be as tall as Raela. And the goblin girl would have short hair and wear a dress.

With an apron. And she would have a cute smile.

As Raela drew the make-
believe girl in the dirt, the
stick hit something hard.

She poked in the soil until she could see
the chain of a necklace. Pulling it from the
ground, she found a pendant
hanging from it.

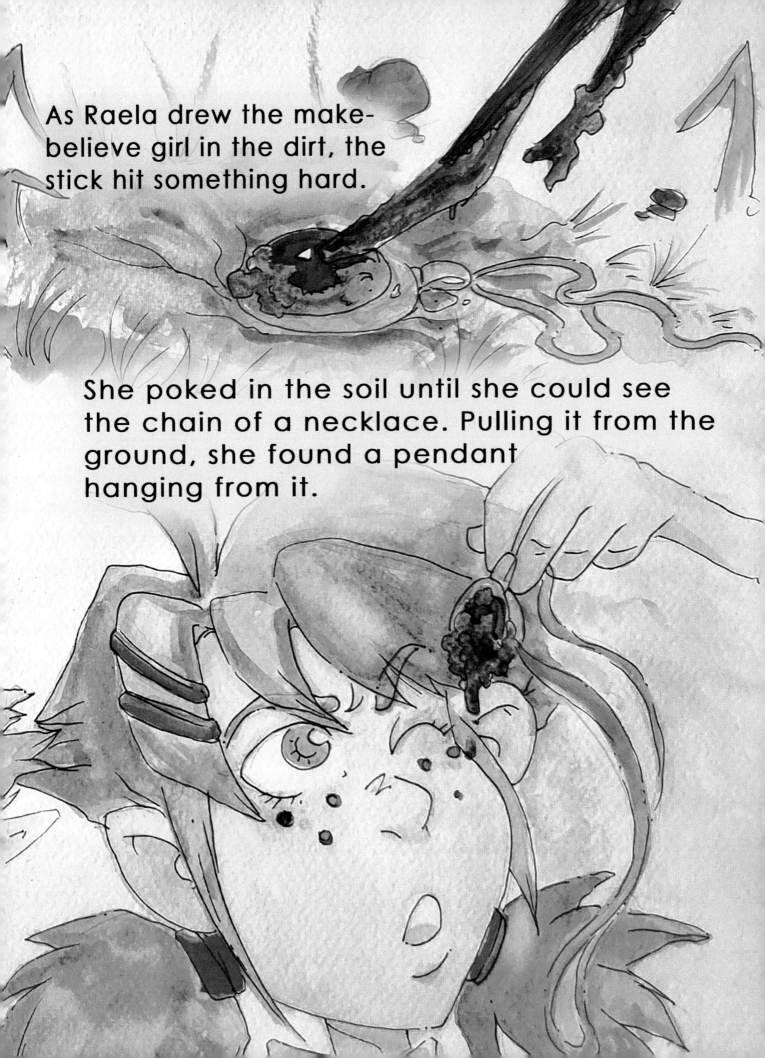

Raela took it to the garden hose next to the cellar and washed off the chain and pendant.

While she worked, she didn't notice the furry figure watching her from the shadows in the nearby bushes.

When she dried the gem with her shirt, the purple stone glimmered.

Raela tilted the gem so the sunshine hit it just right. The pendant began to glow.

On the wooden slats of the dirty old cellar, a doorway appeared. It looked like a wall of water.

This is just what I have always dreamed of, Raela thought.

She was going
to have a real
adventure!

Raela slipped the
necklace over her
head.

Then she stepped through the watery gateway.

On the other side, Raela was surprised to find she wasn't wet. Looking around, she found herself in a forest.

Peeking at her through the trees was a unicorn.

Raela was definitely having an adventure!

She followed the mythical creature
into the trees, hoping to touch it.

But the unicorn ran off.

Raela glanced around for the wall of water. It was gone. How would she get back home?

A shiver went down her back like it did when someone was watching her.

"Who are you?" a girl's voice asked.

Raela spun around and found
the goblin girl she had
sketched in the dirt earlier.

"Wow. Are you an elf?"
Raela moved closer.

"No! I'm a goblin.

She stretched her hand
toward Raela.

"What are you?" the goblin girl asked.

Raela counted the fingers on Zel's hand and held out her own.

"You have six fingers!" Raela said.

"And you only have five. Did you lose one?"

Raela grinned. "No. Our hands and ears grow this way."

Zel's eyes glowed with excitement. "My little sister Raven will not believe I met you. Come with me, so I can prove to her you're real."

"Come with you where?

"To my house," Zel said.

The sun dipped behind the trees, and Raela wondered what time it was. She didn't want to get into trouble back home.

"Please," Zel begged. "We will only stay a few minutes. Then I'll show you the way back."

You know the way to the water wall?

"The Portal? Of course!"

It was growing darker. Raela had that feeling again that someone—or something—was watching them.

Raela decided she was done with this adventure for now.

"I need to go home," she said.

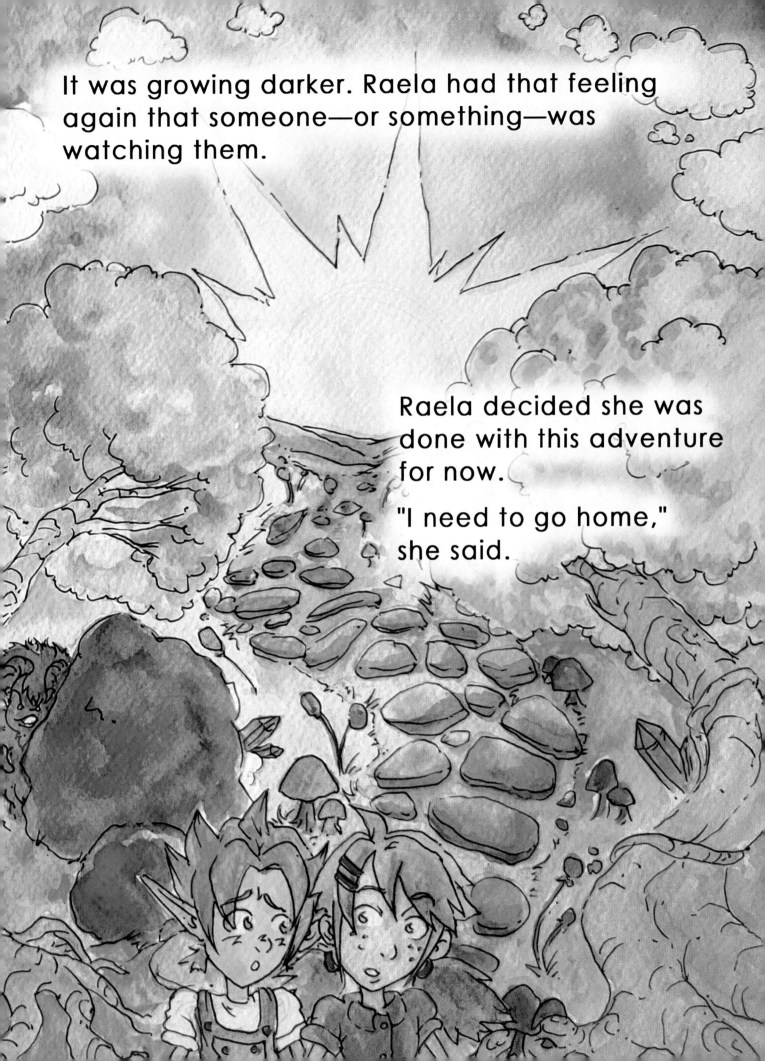

"Will you come back?" Zel wore a pouty face, and Raela felt bad for her.

"Yes. Tomorrow. Please take me to the portal."

"Okay. This way."

A shadowy figure covered in fur burst from the bushes.

Screaming, the girls dashed through the forest.

To the side came a flicker of light. The girls ran to it. When they barged through the bushes, they saw the portal in the last rays of the setting sun.

"There it is," Zel cried.

At the sound of something crashing behind them, the girls dashed to the watery wall. They turned to face the furry creature, but it stopped just outside the light.

"You have to leave," Zel yelled.

"Will you be safe?" Raela asked, looking worriedly at the furry creature and the dimming sunlight.

"There's another way I can go."

"See you tomorrow," Raela cried as Zel pushed her through the portal.

When Raela landed in her own world, she found the sun was going down there too. As the rays of the sun disappeared, so did the portal.

She ran into her house and found Pearl still talking on her phone.

Raela went to the window and looked at the dim form of the cellar wall. She felt the necklace still around her neck. Maybe she needed both light and the pendant to make the portal work.

Tomorrow, Raela would bring a flashlight.

Made in the USA
Monee, IL
09 April 2025

15466916R00021